This book is dedicated to all the children of the Black diaspora,
both young and old. It was written by **us**, illustrated by **us**
and born out of love for **us** – D.A.

PUFFIN BOOKS

UK | USA | Canada | Ireland | Australia | India | New Zealand | South Africa

Puffin Books is part of the Penguin Random House group of companies
whose addresses can be found at global.penguinrandomhouse.com.

www.penguin.co.uk   www.puffin.co.uk   www.ladybird.co.uk

First published 2021

001

Text copyright © Dapo Adeola, 2021
Illustrations copyright © Dapo Adeola, Alyissa Johnson, Sharee Miller, Jade Orlando, Diane Ewen,
Reggie Brown, Onyinye Iwu, Chanté Timothy, Gladys Jose, Bex Glendining, Joelle Avelino,
Dunni Mustapha, Nicole Miles, Charlot Kristensen, Kingsley Nebechi, Camilla Sucre,
Derick Brooks, Jobe Anderson, Selom Sunu, 2021
The moral right of the author and illustrators has been asserted

Printed in Italy

The authorized representative in the EEA is Penguin Random House Ireland,
Morrison Chambers, 32 Nassau Street, Dublin D02 YH68

A CIP catalogue record for this book is available from the British Library

ISBN: 978–0–241–52194–6

All correspondence to: Puffin Books, Penguin Random House Children's
One Embassy Gardens, 8 Viaduct Gardens, London SW11 7BW

HEY YOU!

HEY YOU!

Written by
DAPO ADEOLA

With illustrations by:

DAPO ADEOLA
ALYISSA JOHNSON
SHAREE MILLER
JADE ORLANDO
DIANE EWEN

REGGIE BROWN
ONYINYE IWU
CHANTÉ TIMOTHY
GLADYS JOSE
BEX GLENDINING
JOELLE AVELINO
DUNNI MUSTAPHA

NICOLE MILES
CHARLOT KRISTENSEN
KINGSLEY NEBECHI
CAMILLA SUCRE
DERICK BROOKS
JOBE ANDERSON
SELOM SUNU

PUFFIN

This book grew out of an emotional response to the events of 2020: the tragic story of George Floyd and the global protests that followed; the mass awakening to the impacts of structural racism. The book also stems from a question my editor asked that struck a deep chord in me:

"When was the first time you felt empowered as a Black person – that you deeply believed you could live your dreams?"

The answer for me was in my mid to late twenties. So much later than I felt it should have been. What might have been different had I felt more confident and assured in my skin at a younger age – if I'd seen my story told?

With that second question in my mind, I set about writing the words I wish I'd heard as a child. As I wrote, the words became both a letter to my past self and also a letter to my future child . . .

When I was growing up, there was a sense that Black people couldn't achieve in creative industries, and there were limited examples of Black success. Black people were rarely at the heart of stories – the hero. I wrote this book in the hope that it might help future generations of Black children to feel empowered and seen. I hope also to inspire Black parents who may have found empowerment in their adult years, but perhaps haven't yet found the words to pass that confidence on to their children. Lastly, I hope to give all children, parents and educators a window into the challenges that so many Black children encounter as they grow up – whether overt or more subtle.

It has been crucial to enlist the help of many different voices in bringing these words to life. As I'm just one person, I can't possibly hope to speak for the entire diaspora. The rich variety of talented illustrators in this book mirrors the rich variety of people that make up the Black diaspora across the globe, and there's something here for all of us.

We hope you enjoy your read.

Dapo Adeola, June 2021

Hey you . . .

Welcome to the world.

We've waited **so** long to meet you –
and, oh, has it been worth it.

I want to let you know our dreams and hopes for you
and the things about life you must always remember . . .

I hope that you know
you are loved . . . **always**.

A love that started long before your birth,
passed on in the very fabric of your being,
from generation to generation.

You are **wonderful**.

I hope that you never lose sight
of the wonder that is you . . .

even though the world won't always let you see it . . .

Love your **beautiful skin**.

Some people believe that one skin colour is better than another.
But they are **so** wrong. Every skin colour has its own unique beauty.

You stand on the shoulders
of **greatness**.

You share your magical melanin with countless
generations of geniuses, creators, leaders
and great thinkers.

Your potential is infinite.

You always have a **choice**.

You are not defined by the views of others –
it's the qualities in you that count.

You choose your own path in life
and you can be whatever you want to be.

Be **curious!**

I hope that you question everything.

Curiosity gives you a special kind of freedom –
the kind of freedom that can't be contained
by pages or walls . . .

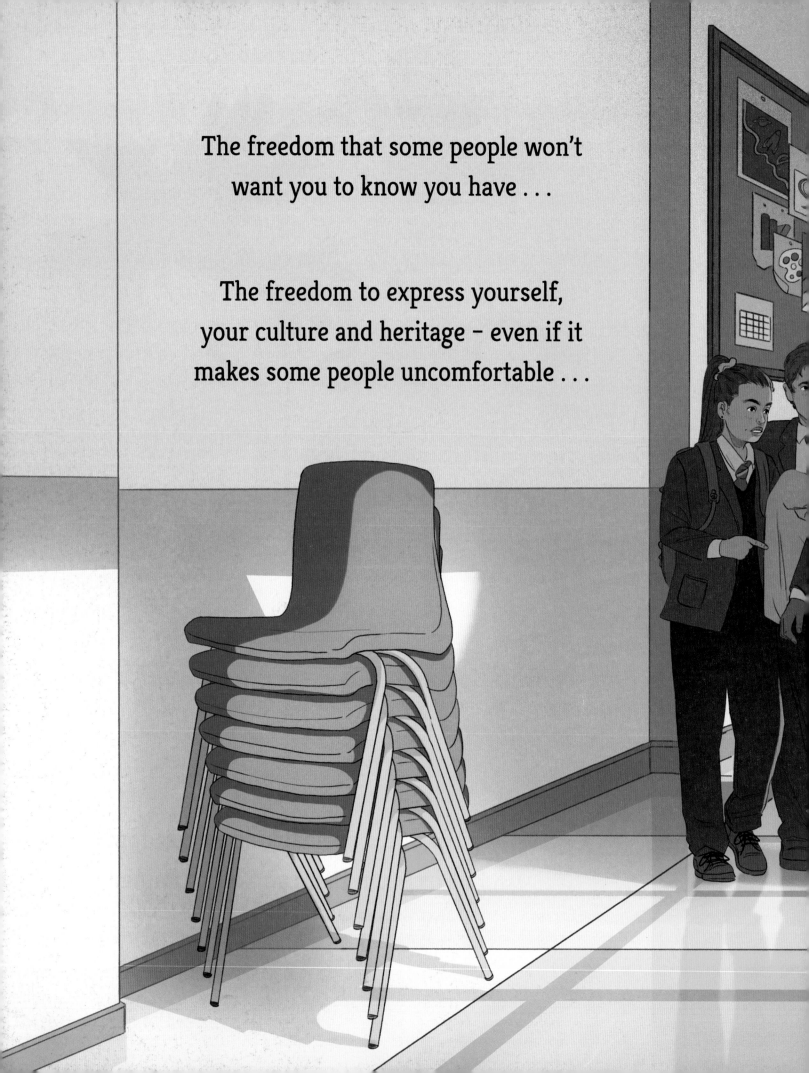

The freedom that some people won't
want you to know you have . . .

The freedom to express yourself,
your culture and heritage – even if it
makes some people uncomfortable . . .

The freedom that allows you to break
through glass ceilings and be yourself,
as there is no one else exactly like you.

Do not be discouraged.
Let your imagination loose and you can
use it to fly wherever you want to go.

Keep searching – you will find
the **right stories** for you.

Stories full of the knowledge
and wisdom of your ancestors.
They travelled their own paths and
still light the way for you and me . . .

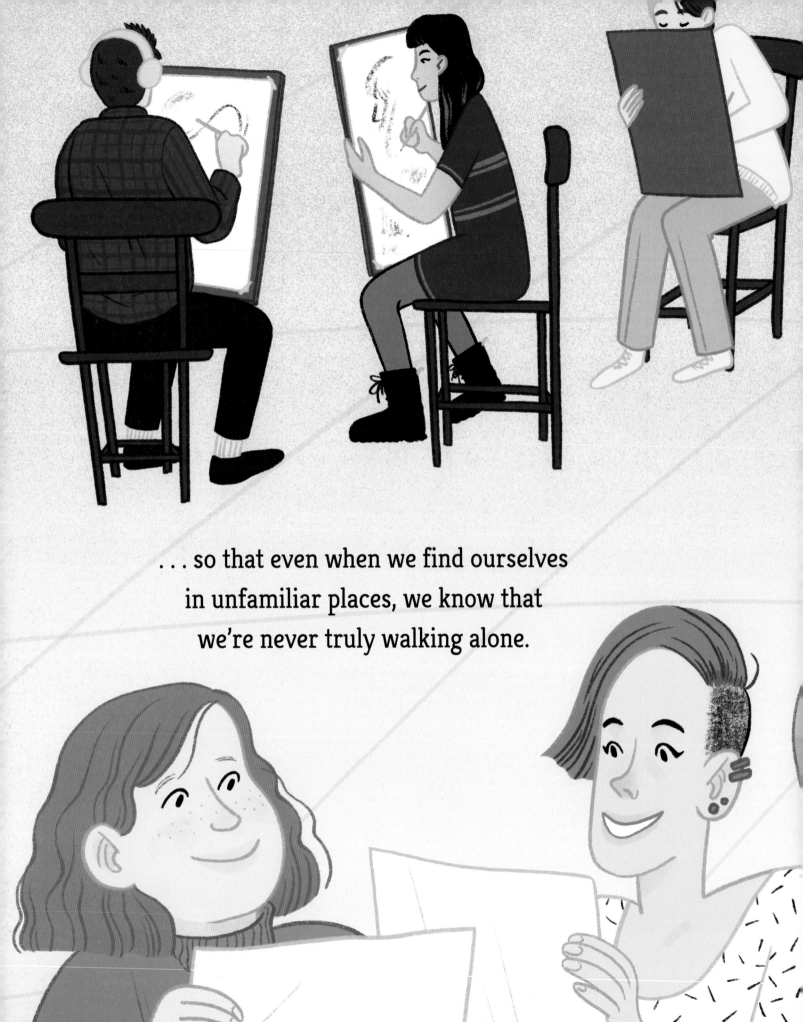

. . . so that even when we find ourselves
in unfamiliar places, we know that
we're never truly walking alone.

Happiness, love and laughter
will find you on your **journey**.

You will meet many different
and incredible people:

friends who will fill
you with joy . . .

and love that lifts
you off the ground.

As Black people we must **work together**.

Wherever we are on this
planet, our joy is shared . . .

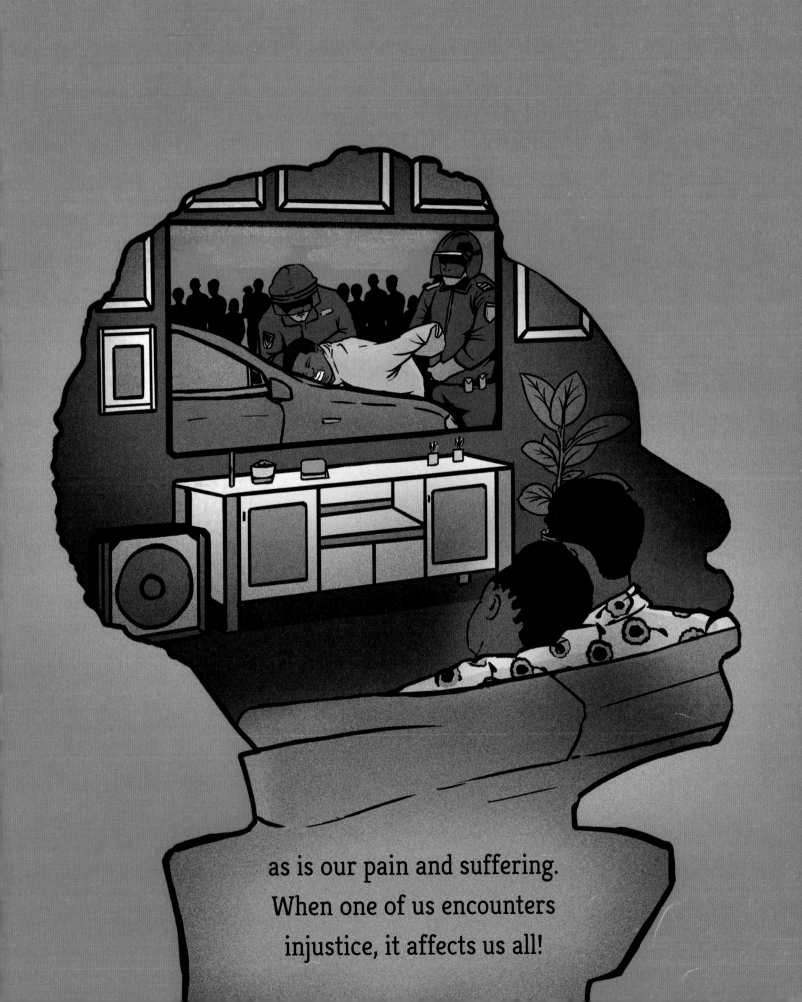

as is our pain and suffering.
When one of us encounters
injustice, it affects us all!

Others will try to tell our stories for us or even erase us from them altogether. We each have the power to create the change we wish to see in the world . . .

You are a
hero.

With your own incredible superpowers, and the love
of your family and friends, you will be unstoppable.

My dream for you is that one day you too will be in a position to **dream for others**.

As you pass the love you have down to
a new generation, I hope they are also
inspired to follow their dreams . . .

And may they be truly **magnificent dreams.**

Hey You! is a collaboration between **Dapo Adeola** and **eighteen talented Black illustrators:**

Alyissa Johnson is a graphic designer and lettering artist who focuses on positivity and feminism. You can find Alyissa playing with her dog Luna or selling prints at a local pop-up shop in Kansas City, Missouri.

Jade Orlando lives in Atlanta, Georgia. When she's not drawing, you can usually find her curled up with her cats and a really good book.

Reggie Brown lives in San Diego, California. He has always loved to draw and can't remember wanting to be anything but an artist. Reggie loves the McRib and wants it back.

Chanté Timothy creates work that explores different themes of diversity and inclusion. She's best known for her debut book *A Black Woman Did That* by Malaika Adero.

Sharee Miller lives on the east coast of America. Her art is fresh, full of joy and encourages all who view it to smile.

Diane Ewen is from the West Midlands in the UK. She has always been in love with art and graduated from the University of Wolverhampton with a B.A. honours degree in illustration.

Onyinye Iwu is a Nigerian illustrator and author. She was born in Italy where she spent her childhood, then moved to the UK. Onyinye enjoys reading books and drawing patterns.

Gladys Jose lives in Orlando, Florida, with her supportive, loving husband, her energetic, brilliant daughter and a very sweet pup named Miles.

Bex Glendining is based in the UK, and has worked on projects such as *Seen: Edmonia Lewis*, *Penultimate Quest*, *Nubia: Real One* and *Lupina*.

Joelle Avelino is a Congolese and Angolan illustrator and animator. Her animation project with Malala Fund was featured in *Design Weekly's* favourite International Women's Day projects of 2020.

Dunni Mustapha grew up in the UK and has always been fascinated by picture books and magazines. She likes using pictures to tell stories and capturing people's quirks and unique traits.

Nicole Miles is an illustrator, cartoonist, hand-letterer and designer from the Bahamas. She currently lives in West Yorkshire in the UK with her pet snake and human boyfriend.

Charlot Kristensen has worked with clients such as Google, *New York Times* and *Huffpost*. Her first graphic novel, *What We Don't Talk About,* was published in 2020.

Kingsley Nebechi is a Nigerian based in London. Crazy for comics, fanatical about films and inspired by African art, Kingsley is recognized for his commercial and gallery work.

Camilla Sucre is a Caribbean American artist born in New York and raised in Baltimore. She studied illustration and film at MICA with a passion for multidisciplinary arts and telling stories.

Derick Brooks is based in Richmond, Virginia and loves to create adventurous stories about Black folk. He lives with his wife and pets, and really loves potatoes.

Jobe Anderson lives in Birmingham in the UK. He loves creating wacky scenarios and making short stories. When he isn't drawing, you'll find him reading comic books and watching movies.

Selom Sunu is based in London. His children's illustration work includes *The Puffin Book of Big Dreams* and *New York Times* bestseller *Ghost* by Jason Reynolds.

WE STAND ON THE SHOULDERS OF GREATNESS!

- **Usain Bolt** is an athlete who made history in 2016 by achieving the Triple Triple – three gold medals at three Olympic Games in a row.

- **Steve McQueen** is a Turner Prize winning film-maker. He was the first Black film-maker to receive the Academy Award for Best Picture for his film *12 Years a Slave*.

- **Malorie Blackman** is an award-winning British author, best known for her critically acclaimed Noughts & Crosses series. She was the Children's Laureate from 2013 to 2015.

- **Janelle Monáe** is a Grammy-nominated singer-songwriter, actor, model and long-time activist for the Black Lives Matter movement.

- **Muhammad Ali** was a boxer, philanthropist and activist. He was the first to win the World Heavyweight Championship three times, earning him the nickname The Greatest.

- **Stevie Wonder** is one of the world's most famous singer-songwriters and musicians. He has been blind since shortly after his birth.

- **Beyoncé Knowles-Carter** is a Grammy award-winning singer-songwriter, director and humanitarian. Her incredible career has spanned over three decades.

- **Michelle Obama** is a lawyer, author and former First Lady of the United States of America. She is an active advocate for children's literacy and women's rights.

- **Barack Obama** served as the 44th President of the United States of America. He set up the Obama Foundation, which provides mentoring and training opportunities for young men of colour.

- **Maya Angelou** was a poet, author and civil rights activist. Her book *I Know Why the Caged Bird Sings* was the first non-fiction bestseller by an African American woman.

- **Fela Kuti** was a pioneering musician and political activist. He used his music to raise awareness for matters that affected both his country, Nigeria, and the continent of Africa.

- **Diane Abbott** is a politician and human rights activist. She was the first Black woman elected to be a Member of Parliament, and is the longest-serving Black MP.

- **Olive Morris** was a community activist who dedicated her life to campaigning for feminism and racial equity. She founded the Brixton Black Women's group in 1973 – one of Britain's first networks to help Black women engage in politics.